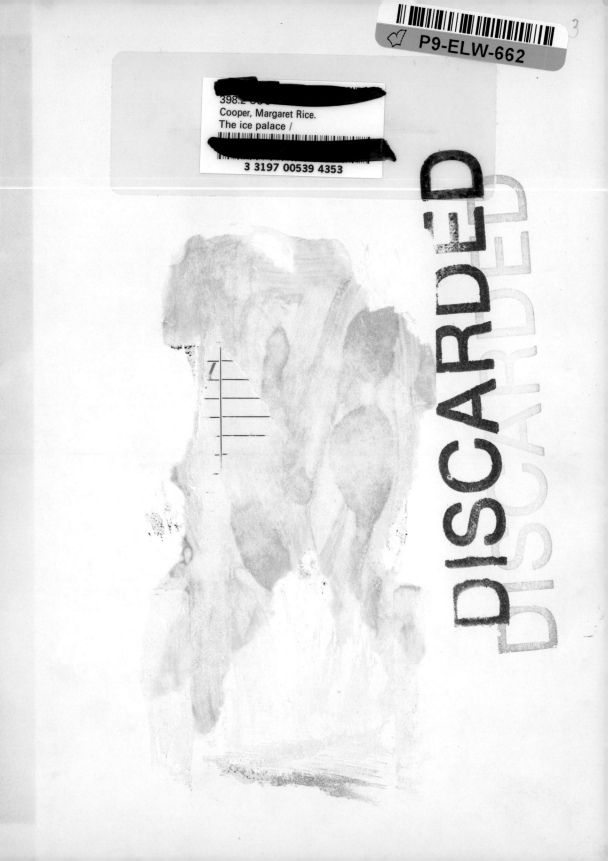

THE ICE PALACE

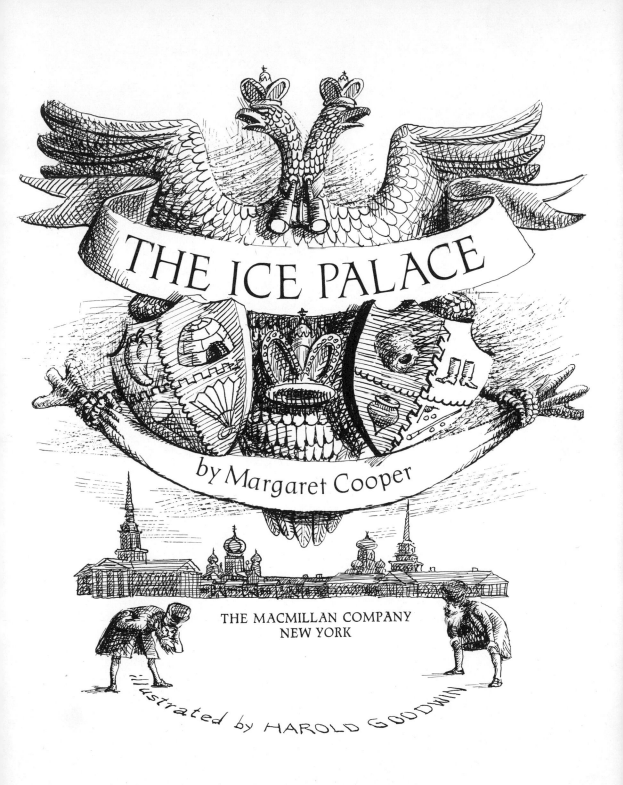

THE ICE PALACE

by Margaret Cooper

THE MACMILLAN COMPANY
NEW YORK

Illustrated by HAROLD GOODWIN

To Princess Georgiana

Once upon a time, in a faraway city, there was a very cold winter. The snow came dancing down from the sky until even the smallest twigs of the bare dark trees turned white. Every roof sparkled, and the palace tower, built like a wedding cake with a dome on top, was covered with snow frosting. Ice appeared as if by magic, making the streets slippery beneath the runners of the jingling horse-drawn sleighs. The snorting horses trotted fast to keep warm, and the passengers bundled themselves up in such tall fur hats, bulging fur coats and great fur mittens that they looked like bears with red-tipped noses. Everything froze so hard that the tall spires of the city glittered like so many upside-down icicles.

Deep in the frozen river that ran past the palace, the fish were complaining.

"The ice is so thick overhead," grumbled a red perch, "that we can't even see what's going on at the palace." The perch thought that only the other fish were listening to what it said, but a fisherman walking on the ice above overheard the remark.

"No view?" said the fisherman to himself. "I'll fix that." And he quickly cut a nice square hole in the ice. The perch couldn't wait to see the outside world and immediately swam into a net the fisherman had lowered into the hole. The other fish clucked their lips, shook their heads wisely and followed into the net.

At the palace, there was grumbling, too. The candles in the beautiful hanging chandeliers of crystal sputtered in the cold. All around the huge mirrored banquet room, finches and larks and nightingales coughed and muttered in their gold cages. The pet rabbit sat in a corner and angrily twitched. The princes and dukes shook in their wigs, shivered in their boots and spun tops to keep warm. The princes had bigger tops than the dukes because they were more important, and the queen had the biggest top of all, covered with green velvet to match her robe. She sat on her throne, sulking under a green silk canopy, her gold binoculars hanging at her side. To keep out the cold, she had taken off her crown containing 2,579 rubies and emeralds and diamonds, and tied a bright red kerchief over her head.

All of a sudden, the head chamberlain rushed into the banquet room.

2

"Here's the soup," he shouted, to make himself heard over the noise of spinning tops. "And you better come and get it while it's hot." There was a scramble of princes and dukes to the long table. The queen slurped the sauerkraut soup with an enormous spoon.

"General," she said sternly, "stop eating out of the tureen. Use your soup plate." The general stood up, saluted, clicked his heels and reached for the caviar.

3

Then silence fell, except for the sound of spoons and slurps.

In the middle of everything, Princess Kasha came thumping into the banquet room in her blue brocade slippers.

"I'm hot," she announced, standing on tiptoe to see whether her face looked red in the mirror.

"HOT??" screamed the court in one voice, and all the princes and dukes dropped their spoons into the tureen with a tremendous clatter. The general was so startled that his little brown wig fell off his big pink head, and he sneezed. "Gesundheit," he said stiffly, and he went off to the stable for a friendly chat with his horses.

"I'm hot," Princess Kasha repeated in a louder voice, and she started toward the outer door. The queen rose to her full height of 6 feet 8 inches. She towered on her throne while the princes and dukes

5

cowered at the table. "You are not leaving this palace without your muff and your boots," she told Princess Kasha severely.

"I'm hot," Princess Kasha said again, not quite so loud. She stamped her foot on the gorgeous Turkey carpet and marched off to her room, sizzling.

"Look, your majesty," said the chamberlain, and he pointed to a neat slipper-shaped hole burned in the gorgeous Turkey carpet.

"Hmmm," muttered the queen, and she sent for the palace Oracle. The Oracle arrived, wearing one beard and carrying another, just in case he needed it to stroke when he was solving a very hard problem. The queen turned her binoculars the wrong way around and looked at the Oracle through them to make him smaller.

"Oracle," she ordered, "find out whether Princess Kasha is really hot."

The Oracle hung his extra beard over the back of a yellow velvet chair and went to see Princess Kasha, who was steaming in her room. He bowed low, walked up to the Princess and touched her forehead.

"Ouch!" he yelled, without meaning to at all, and quite soon there was a blister on his middle finger. He bowed low again and returned to the banquet room, licking his finger.

"Well?" asked the queen. "Is she hot or isn't she?"

"She's as hot as Tuesday," said the Oracle. Tuesday was usually the hottest day of the week. "All right," said the queen, "since you're such a good Oracle, tell me how to cool her off." The Oracle grabbed his extra beard and stroked it for all he was worth, while the court waited breathlessly to hear what he would say. Even the finches and larks and nightingales in their gold cages stopped muttering.

Then a finch accidentally coughed very loud, and the Oracle stopped stroking his extra beard.

"I need four messengers," he said gravely. The whole court breathed a big sigh of relief.

"Very well," the queen agreed. She clapped her hands four times and the four messengers appeared in long black cloaks.

"You are to go to the four ends of the earth," said the Oracle to the messengers, "and find out how extra-hot people get cool. And you are to be back immediately with the news."

The four messengers bowed low and disappeared into their long black cloaks. The first messenger jumped on the back of the East Wind, which blew him West in a great tempest. The second messenger put on his magic ski shoes and tracked North in no time at all. The third messenger was going South, and he had an easy trip, because he could slide downhill all the way. The fourth messenger grabbed a passing lightning bolt and reached East almost before he started.

While the messengers were gone, the princes and dukes decided to go outdoors and play on the toboggan slide, even though it was such a freezing, icy, blustery, snowy day. They put on their tall fur hats, their bulging fur coats and their great fur mittens, and out they went, leaving the queen alone with her pet rabbit and the Oracle.

"Amuse me," she ordered the Oracle. He sat down on one of the yellow velvet chairs and gazed sadly at the pet rabbit.

"It is said of this city, your majesty," he told the queen, "that it has on one side the sea, on the other sorrow, on the third moss and on the fourth a sigh."

It took the queen exactly twenty-two minutes to decide whether the Oracle had amused her. By that time, the rabbit was asleep, the Oracle had gone out to play with the princes and dukes and the messengers had reappeared, breathless and red in the face. Each one of them pulled an enormous roll of paper out of his cloak. The Oracle came rushing into the banquet room, scattering snow all over the gorgeous Turkey carpet, and grabbed his extra beard. The court came back from the toboggan slide.

The first messenger unrolled his piece of paper and studied it. He turned it around and he turned it over, then he looked through it at the light. Finally, he announced, "In the West, when people are hot, they take a thing that looks like a witch's hat upside down and fill it with something very cold and creamy. The some-

thing cold and creamy comes in many different colors: pink, green, orange, brown and vanilla. They say they feel much cooler after they eat it."

"Chamberlain," ordered the queen, "send for the chef." The chef arrived instantly, quaking from head to toe.

"Go back to your kitchen," the queen ordered him, "fill a witch's hat upside down with something very cold and creamy and give it to Princess Kasha."

The chef gasped his way back to the kitchen and slumped into a chair. He knew how to make a witch's hat out of sugar—in fact he had done it dozens of times to decorate sugar witches for birthday cakes—but where could he find something very cold and creamy? His eyes wandered all over the kitchen, but nothing would do; not the dried beans, not the bacon, not the cabbage, not the butter, not even the caviar. Finally, he looked out the window, and stopped slumping.

A few minutes later, he was serving Princess Kasha a delicious ice cream cone made of vanilla-flavored snow ice cream. By then the princess had thumped down from her room again and was standing in the middle of the banquet room, still steaming. Her eyes lit up when she saw the ice cream cone, and she ate it in only four gulps, while the court, as usual, waited breathlessly.

"Yum," she said to the chef, but she stayed as hot as ever.

The second messenger had somehow got wrapped up in his roll of paper, so the third messenger stepped up and made his announcement.

"In the South, when people are hot, they eat something red and hot-peppery called chili, and then they're chilly, too."

"Very puzzling," said the queen and sent for the chef again. He was soon trying to serve Princess Kasha a bowl of hot, peppery chili, set on a large silver platter. But she turned up her pretty nose.

"I hate red, and I hate pepper, and I know because I never tasted it," she said flatly, and she stayed as hot as ever.

The second messenger was still all wrapped up, struggling to get loose, and the fourth messenger was bursting to speak.

"In the East," he announced, talking very fast, "when people are hot, they sit down on a chair and wave something back and forth in front of themselves." The queen knew all about fans, but she was ready to try anything, and she ordered the biggest one in the palace to be brought to Princess Kasha. The princess really enjoyed fanning herself, especially when she snapped the huge fan shut with a bang to make the Oracle jump. But she stayed as hot as ever.

Now the second messenger finally got himself unwrapped.

"In the North," he announced proudly, "people are

not usually hot. Even so, they live in smooth round houses like beehives, made of ice and snow, and I'm sure it is very cool inside."

"This calls for the general," said the queen. The general came in from the stable with his little brown wig slipping to one side of his big pink head, and his jacket missing a button.

"General, we must build a snow beehive for Princess Kasha, to cool her off," said the queen. The general sneezed politely and mobilized the army.

A regiment of soldiers worked for ten days and nights without stopping and built a smooth round igloo of snow blocks just big enough to hold the princess. The princess gathered up all her dolls and made

ready with great glee to move in, but the queen inspected the igloo through the palace window, using her binoculars turned the right way around, and she wouldn't allow such a thing.

"Beautiful as it is," she declared, "no princess of mine can live in such a small house. We must have an ice palace." So while Princess Kasha steamed in fury the queen got off her throne and went to find the experts.

The experts were in the royal billiards room.

"It's my turn," the queen announced grandly as she swept in, her green velvet cloak billowing behind her, and snatched a billiards cue. The queen was an excellent billiards player.

"Now," she said, briskly chalking her cue, "since you're all such good billiards players, let's see how good you are at building an ice palace. Princess Kasha is hot, and we have to cool her off." She paused a moment and then added, "And mind you finish it by the princess' birthday next week." With that she made a terrific three-cushion shot and gave her cloak an extra billow as she swept out of the room. The experts put down their cues, stretched out on the billiards table and called a meeting to decide how to build the ice palace.

First they elected a Chairman, who got off the table and sat on a chair. Then they elected a Secretary, who took out his watch and read the minutes. He read that it was fourteen minutes later than it should be, so there was nothing to do but call off the meeting, go on with the billiards game and hope for an idea. But while the others were picking up their cues, one expert continued to lie stretched out on the billiards table.

"Gentlemen," he said, opening his eyes and sitting up, "while you have been at your important meeting,

I have had an important sleep, and I have dreamed of the ice palace." With that, he leaped off the billiards table, chalked a cue, then used it to draw a chalk picture of a dazzling ice palace on the dark-green cloth of the billiards table.

But, beautiful as it was, the experts didn't know how to build the ice palace, so they put on their tall fur caps with bells and they went to the stable to see the general.

"General," said the expert Secretary, "we must build an ice palace to cool off Princess Kasha. You built such a beautiful igloo that you're just the person to carry out our plan. But it has to be finished by the princess' birthday." The general sneezed pleasantly and mobilized the navy.

The navy came out of the Admiralty on the other side of the river and marched across the ice, ready for action. The sailors looked very stylish in their smart black boots with white stockings and their dark-green tunics with wide red sashes and wide red ties. The commodore led the march, looking even more stylish because his black boots were shiny and he wore a green cocked hat with a very large white feather. When the commodore reached the general, the general bowed so low that the top of his little brown wig almost touched the ice. The commodore lost no time bowing—he was much too stylish for that—but continued his march. His step was so crisp that even the fish down in the river knew something unusual was about to happen.

"What do you think they're up to now?" a sturgeon muttered darkly. "They're always meddling. Never content to stay indoors like sensible people when it's freezing cold up there."

Unlike fishermen, who listen to what fish have to say, the commodore had other things on his mind. First he marched to the royal billiards room and examined the experts' drawing, nodding his head so that the very large white feather waved up and down. Then he marched back to the middle of the river, halfway between the palace and the Admiralty, whipped a ruler out of his back pocket, measured his shiny black

boot, and paced off the space for the ice palace. Then he blew his silver whistle, and 374 sailors came running over the ice.

"Sailors," said the commodore, "the ice palace will be built on this spot. Now go and get the ice." The 374 sailors ran along the frozen river until they found a place where the ice was smooth and clear. Then each sailor whipped a ruler out of his back pocket and began to measure. They measured and measured, and when they had enough ice blocks marked out with their rulers, the commodore suddenly arrived, riding on a horse-drawn plow. On the horse's head he had put a very large white feather that waved as the horse pulled the plow over all the marks and snorted to keep warm.

When the plow had cut along the marks to make grooves, each of the 374 sailors whipped a handsaw out of his back pocket and began to saw. They sawed along the grooves, without stopping even for a snack, until the ice blocks were all cut.

The fish were furious about the noise.

"Nobody can sleep a wink around here," the sturgeon grumbled, and steered itself upriver to find some peace and quiet.

The commodore came back, carrying 374 crowbars in one hand and lunch for everybody and a samovar in the other. Very quickly, with one eye on lunch, the sailors pried the ice blocks loose from the frozen river and loaded them on sleds to be taken to the building site. The commodore handed around the rolls and glasses of steaming tea, fresh from the samovar, and everybody relaxed.

While they were relaxing, Princess Kasha was making a small scene at the palace. She demanded another ice cream cone, even though she had already eaten sixty-two since breakfast, and the chef was running out of flavors. He had tried raspberry-butterscotch, strawberry-mint, pistachio-fudge and licorice-walnut, and now he was beside himself. His eyes wandered around the kitchen, and, as usual, nothing would do: not the sausages, not the tea, not the herring, not the pickled apples. Just in time, his eyes fell on the leftover sauerkraut soup. The princess was so pleased with her sauerkraut-flavored ice cream cone that she actually said "Yum" twice.

The 374 sailors finished relaxing and began to work furiously. Soon the ice palace could be seen rising, block by block. That is, everybody but the queen could see it rising; she had decided not to look. But if the queen had looked, she would have seen half the sailors hauling the great bluish ice blocks and raising them into place with hoisting cranes. And if she had listened, she would have heard a shout from the commodore, who was standing on top of a big snow pile to direct the work.

"Use water as cement," he advised in a loud voice, waving his cocked hat to attract attention. Fourteen sailors immediately whipped buckets out of their back pockets and formed a bucket brigade. Because of the freezing, icy, blustery cold, the water froze the moment it was poured over the ice blocks and stuck them together perfectly.

All around the rising ice palace, little groups of sailors were doing special jobs. Some were making ice furniture, shaping the ice into tables and chairs and sofas. Some were sculptors, using their chisels and lathes and polishers to make statues of ice, and some worked on outdoor things. One group specialized in doors and windows. They found some very thin, clear ice for the windowpanes, so that Princess Kasha would be able to enjoy the view. At the moment, she was in

her room, as hot as ever, giving all her dolls an iced-tea party.

The sailors went on with their work. There were ice-plant specialists and ice-animal specialists, ice-roof specialists and ice-fireplace specialists. There were also ice-food specialists, working for all they were worth to stock the ice larder. The commodore stood on top of

his snow pile directing everything for so many hours that his cocked hat almost froze to his head and the white feather got too stiff with cold to wave. Darkness fell, but that didn't stop the work. Each of the 374 sailors whipped a candle out of his back pocket and continued with what he was doing.

The queen lit an immense taper, put on her tall fur crown and walked out to inspect the ice palace. She summoned the expert Secretary.

"What do the minutes say?" she demanded. The Secretary pulled out his watch and it immediately froze. Quaking, he said, "It's five and a half minutes later than it should be, and it always will be from now on."

"Very well," said the queen, "then the ice palace will be finished in time."

The queen was right. Exactly as the palace clocks struck midnight to signal the beginning of birthday-dom for the princess, the ice palace was finished. The 374 sailors breathed such a loud sigh of relief that it blew out all their candles and they had to go home in the dark. The commodore groped his way down from his snow pile and rushed indoors to thaw his white feather.

Princess Kasha, who had fallen asleep with a glass of iced tea in her hand, didn't hear the clocks strike.

But when she woke up in the morning, her dolls were lined up in their party clothes, waiting to wish her a happy birthday. Next the queen came bursting in, all excited, wearing her solid-gold nightgown and her red kerchief.

"Happy birthday, my dear," she said, and she pulled back the curtains at the window.

Princess Kasha looked out and was amazed. There in the middle of the river stood the ice palace, blue and sparkling, much more beautiful than any real stone palace could ever be. Rushing past the queen, the princess dashed out of the room and down the stairs in her bare feet. She had to see the ice palace instantly.

The queen reached for her binoculars. "Chamberlain!" she shouted, "I told that princess she wasn't to leave this palace without her muff and her boots, and I meant it, birthday or no birthday." The chamberlain ran after the princess to stop her at the door; he woke the experts; he even called the general, who firmly sneezed, said "Gesundheit" and mobilized both the army *and* the navy. It was no use. Princess Kasha ran faster than any of them, and she got to the ice palace first, in her bare feet.

She reached the solid-ice balustrade surrounding the ice palace, with the chamberlain, the experts, the army and the navy at her heels. Stopping just long enough to notice the handsome square pillars of the balustrade, she rushed behind it.

"Now nobody can come any farther," she said, catching her breath and kicking one bare foot, "because it's *my* birthday and *my* ice palace. I won't let anybody in but my dolls. So there."

Nevertheless, the commodore was standing at the ice-palace door, looking more stylish than ever and waiting to take the princess on a tour of inspection.

"Welcome to the ice palace, Princess Kasha," he said and bowed stiffly as he whipped a guidebook out of his back pocket. With another bow, he turned his back on the princess, opened the guidebook and read aloud:

"The ice palace is 56 feet long, 18 feet wide and 21 feet high."

Princess Kasha gave a large steamy yawn.

"I'm hot," she said. "Let's go inside."

The commodore paid no attention.

"You will notice that the door and window frames seem to be made of green marble," he read from the guidebook. "This is an illusion, as they are actually painted ice."

Princess Kasha interrupted rudely, "Anyone can see that. Who needs an old guidebook to tell you?" As the commodore simply settled his cocked hat more firmly on his head and prepared to continue his reading, the princess decided she had had enough and marched through the ice-palace door.

Immediately she began to feel cooler and her temper began to improve. "What fun," she said to herself and skipped through the hall to the living room. She ran right over to the ice table in the middle of the room, to look at the ice clock and its ice clockwork inside. While she was trying to decide which hand told hours and which told minutes, the commodore came up behind her.

"The table is partially supported," he read, "by a seated ice statue, and next to the sofas . . ." Princess Kasha didn't hear a word, because she had just noticed that some of the princes and dukes had left their calling cards frozen into the tabletop.

"I really must ask them to my birthday party," she said to herself, feeling better and better as she felt cooler and cooler. Then she raced across the room to look at the things the sailor specialists had made to put in the ice cabinet. Tucked away in one corner, behind the ice cups and saucers and dishes and cakes—all painted to look real—the princess could see an ice cream cone that the chef had thoughtfully left for her as a birthday treat. She decided to save it for later.

While the commodore kept right on reading his guidebook, Princess Kasha darted across the hall into the bedroom. It delighted her so much that she hopped up and down on the ice floor in her bare feet.

"Commodore," she cried happily, "stop your reading and send for the queen. And send for my boots, too. It's *cold* in here."

"Cold!" the commodore yelled. "Then the ice palace is a success!" For a wonderful minute, he completely forgot he was so stylish and not only tossed his cocked hat in the air, feather and all, but hopped up and down next to Princess Kasha. Then he went to

fetch the queen. She arrived to find the princess jump-
ing on the big ice bed with its tall canopy and curtains
and pillows with nightcaps on them—all made of ice.
In her hand, the queen personally carried Princess
Kasha's boots and a brand-new birthday muff.

32

The princess jumped off the ice bed and flung her arms around the queen.

"What a wonderful ice palace," she said delightedly. "My dolls are going to have the best winter of their lives. And please kiss me happy birthday now because I'm all cool."

"Cool, indeed," said the queen when the happy-birthday kissing was over, "you're freezing, child. Put on your boots and muff this minute. What's more, we're going to have a fire." The commodore, always alert, lit the ice logs in the ice fireplace. Princess Kasha frowned.

"Ice can't burn," she said, looking straight at the commodore. "You must be cheating." The commodore closed his guidebook and blushed. "It's not really cheating," he murmured to himself, "to pour oil over the ice logs so that the fireplace will work."

Outside, the princes and dukes, the army and navy and the Oracle had all gathered to greet the princess. As she left the bedroom and came to the door, six ice cannon and two ice mortars, all beautifully mounted, fired a salute with real gunpowder. Snuggling into her

new birthday muff and her boots, Princess Kasha bowed as if she were a real, grown-up queen. The commodore, of course, seized the moment of silence to get out his guidebook again; the truth was that he had written it himself and loved it dearly. "Here," he read, "you will observe several trees made entircly of ice, with each leaf separately shaped." For once, Princess Kasha listened, and she saw that the trees even had ice birds perched among the branches.

But suddenly she remembered the ice cream cone in the living-room cabinet, and she dashed back into the ice palace to get it. As she ran across the living room she thought she heard a noise under the floor. Sure enough, the fish were complaining again, deep in the river.

"Some people have all the luck," growled that same

cross sturgeon. "Nobody ever gave *me* a palace for *my* birthday, and I know she's going to have a party, too." Princess Kasha put her mouth down to the floor.

"You know right," she called down through the ice, "and maybe if you stop being so nosy, I'll invite you." Then she took her ice cream cone out of the cabinet— it was her favorite, sauerkraut—and started back across the river to put on her party dress.

All day long there was a bustle at the palace. The princes and dukes had to put on their best yellow and pink and sky-blue party coats; most of the coats were too tight or the cuffs were too short or the buttons were the wrong color. The princesses and duchesses were invited, too, and they had to be laced into their

gold and silver and emerald-green party dresses, and then they had to stand up for the rest of the day to make sure the dresses wouldn't get wrinkled. Princess Kasha chose her best silver taffeta party dress, and over it she wore a transparent white jumper embroidered with beautiful flowers. The Oracle wore both his beards, the commodore carefully brushed his white feather and the general carried his pearl-handled riding whip and perched a new little yellow wig on his big pink head.

Wearing her red kerchief *and* her crown with the 2,579 rubies and emeralds and diamonds, the queen presided at the banquet. She sat under her green silk canopy, where she could see to it that the princes and dukes minded their manners. Most of them were careful to use their spoons and forks because they knew it was such a special party, and only one had to be reminded not to be so greedy. And Princess Kasha was allowed to bring all her dolls to the table in honor of her birthday.

The chef himself brought in the birthday cake,
seven feet around, with silver frosting and a tiny sugar
ice palace on top. After the princess had blown out the

300 candles in one breath, and after everyone had eaten one of the 300 slices of cake, the queen clapped her hands.

"General," she ordered, "it's time to turn on the Northern Lights." Much too polite to sneeze and say "Gesundheit" at a party, the general got up and did as he was asked, without mobilizing either the army or the navy. Then he waved his pearl-handled riding whip and danced off to the stable, his new little yellow wig slipping every which way on his big pink head.

The guests went out onto the frozen river to watch the Northern Lights flicker white and red. Princess Kasha took along her dolls in a huge doll carriage with runners and arranged them in rows to see the entertainment. When everybody was ready, the queen took Princess Kasha by the hand and led her to a spot near the ice palace where lights were glowing. Walking nearer, Princess Kasha could see that candles were shining through a great ice elephant, as big as life, with an elegant ice rider on top.

"Look at his ears!" she cried gleefully. She rushed over to pat it and announced, "I want a ride right now."

The queen clapped her hands and the chamberlain

came running with a velvet-covered ladder. Princess Kasha threw her new birthday muff on the ice, climbed the ladder and took her seat in front of the ice rider. As she leaned forward to admire the elephant's big ears, it sprayed a pretty jet of fire through its trunk, way up into the air, and let out a loud trumpeting noise.

In fact, the ice elephant trumpeted so loudly—with
the help of a man hidden inside—that Princess Kasha
squealed with delight, the Oracle jumped four feet in
the air and lost his extra beard and the experts came
rushing out of the billiards room in a body. They
carried the Chairman in his chair, and he had a lovely
ride until the expert Chair Carriers slipped on the ice.
There they all sprawled.

Princess Kasha gave the elephant a last pat and came down the ladder. The queen clapped her hands again. The general galloped out of the stable, cracked his riding whip and the Northern Lights went out.

Then suddenly, out of the darkness, the ice palace was aglow with thousands of candles. They shone through the walls and the roof so that the whole ice palace glittered like a huge jewel. And they shone through the windows, which the sailor specialists had secretly covered with thin silk screens, beautifully decorated. Figures of lords and ladies and giants seemed to dance on the screens as the candles flickered behind them, lighting the brilliant colors of their costumes. Best of all was the window that showed a little princess holding a muff in one hand and an ice cream cone in the other.

"Come," said the queen, and she led Princess Kasha toward the ice palace. As they approached, two marvelous ice dolphins with curled-up tails sprayed streams of fire from their mouths. And fireworks lit up the sky so that the leaves of the ice trees sparkled and the ice birds on the branches seemed to have feathers of gorgeous colors.

The queen and the princess stood grandly in the ice-

palace doorway while the army and navy marched past. Leading the army, the general felt so important that he sneezed and his little yellow wig fell right off, but he left it on the ice and marched smartly along, his bare pink head shining in the candlelight. The princes and dukes stood by and were dazzled. The princesses and duchesses, who usually chattered without stopping, couldn't say a word.

Princess Kasha was so excited and happy that she got very sleepy all at once. As the last soldier marched past, she ran away from the ice palace and climbed into the carriage with runners, squeezing in next to the dolls.

"Well," said the queen, "I guess there's nothing to do but wheel her home, just as if she were a little tiny thing instead of a great big birthday girl." And she

46

pushed Princess Kasha back to the palace in the carriage on runners, just as if she were an ordinary mother instead of a big fierce queen, 6 feet 8 inches tall.

Next morning, Princess Kasha put on her boots and her new birthday muff without even being asked and wheeled all her dolls out to the ice palace for a tea party with *hot* tea. The dolls loved it, and just as the princess had predicted, they all had the best winter of their lives.

When spring finally came and the freezing, icy, blustery, snowy winter was over, the jingling sleighs vanished and the rolling carriages appeared. The princes and dukes put away their tall fur hats and bulging fur coats and great fur mittens, and their red-tipped noses thawed completely. The queen put her red kerchief in mothballs, clapped her hands and summoned the expert Secretary.

"Get out your watch, Secretary," she said, "and you will see that it is now neither earlier nor later than it should be." The Secretary got out his watch and it immediately thawed. That was the signal. The sun came out and shone very brightly, and the ice palace melted, leaving behind just enough blocks to put in the real-palace cellar so that the chef could make Princess Kasha's ice cream cones all summer.

That is the end of the story about Princess Kasha, who was a fairy-tale princess and who lived happily ever after. But . . . Once upon a time, in the beautiful city of St. Petersburg, there was a very cold winter. The time was the year 1740, St. Petersburg was then the new capital of Russia and a very unusual queen named Empress Anna Ivanovna sat on the throne. Sometimes she wore a crown containing 2,579 rubies and emeralds and diamonds, and sometimes she wore a bright red kerchief. And she was an expert billiards player. Her court was very strange, too; her favorite courtier, a German, was quite a lot like the general, only meaner; it was said that he treated men like horses and horses like men. And the princes and dukes spun tops, played on the toboggan slide and wore pink coats and funny wigs that didn't fit.

In the icy, freezing, blustery, snowy month of January, when the temperature dropped way below zero, Empress Anna ordered an ice palace to be built for the entertainment of her court. It rose block by block in the middle of the frozen river Neva, halfway between the Winter Palace with its wedding-cake tower and the Admiralty with its tall thin spire.

Not only the ice palace itself, but all the ice furniture, the ice
fireplace with the fire, the ice trees with every leaf shaped
separately, the ice dolphins spraying fire and even the ice
elephant were really there. And the engravings of the ice
palace that appear on this and the preceding page were
actually drawn in 1740 by a man who saw it with his own eyes
before spring gave the
signal and the
ice palace
melted.